A Day with Parkinson's

BEST GRANDPA EVER

A. Hultquist

pictures by
Joanne Lew-Vriethoff

Albert Whitman & Company
Chicago, Illinois

To all the families who are and have been
affected by Parkinson's—JLV

Thank you to Lisa Kokontis, MD,
and to Nicholas Jasinski, PsyD, for their expertise.

Library of Congress Cataloging-in-Publication
data is on file with the publisher.

Text copyright © 2016 by A. Hultquist
Pictures copyright © 2016 by Albert Whitman & Company
Pictures by Joanne Lew-Vriethoff
Published in 2016 by Albert Whitman & Company
ISBN 978-0-8075-5581-1

Printed in China
10 9 8 7 6 5 4 3 2 1 HH 24 23 22 21 20 19 18 17 16 15
Design by Jordan Kost

For more information about Albert Whitman & Company,
visit our web site at www.albertwhitman.com.

Noah and his mom were visiting Grandpa for the weekend.
"Today's the day we're going to the beach!" Mom called.
"Go see if Grandpa's awake."

Noah ran to his grandfather's bedroom, where he found him massaging his left foot. The toes were curled under and Grandpa was trying to relax the muscles to straighten them out.

"Today's beach day!"

"I know, buddy," his grandpa said. "We're going to have fun." He didn't look very happy. In fact, his face didn't look either happy or sad, but Noah knew he was excited. His grandpa loved the beach.

Noah's grandfather got his toes uncurled and slowly walked across the room toward the bathroom where he kept his morning pills. He lost his balance and stumbled. Noah was afraid he might fall. But his grandpa grabbed on to a chair to steady himself.

When his grandpa walked into the kitchen a few minutes later, Noah noticed that his left hand was shaking.

"Did you take your medication?" Mom asked.

"Yup. I should be better pretty soon," Grandpa replied.

Noah watched his grandfather try not to spill any juice in his shaking hand as he read the news. He thought about how his grandpa had changed since he developed Parkinson's.

His grandpa was usually the first one up in the morning so he could exercise and take a shower before breakfast.

He still exercised every day, but some days he moved more slowly, and he had to wait for his pills to kick in.

By the time his grandfather finished breakfast and reading the news, his medicine was working. He smiled and said, "Let's get going!"

"Hooray!" Noah yelled.

Noah, Mom, and Grandpa got on their bikes and pedaled toward the beach. When they arrived, they locked up their bikes and walked along the boardwalk.

When they reached the end, Noah was about to run down to the beach when his grandfather suddenly stopped walking and stood still.

"Looks like I'm frozen," he said.

Noah knew this meant his grandpa couldn't get his feet to move. Noah also knew he shouldn't help him unless his grandpa asked.

"Can you help me out, buddy?" Grandpa asked.

Noah knew just what to do. He drew a line in the sand in front of his grandfather's feet. "Okay," he said, "move your foot backward first and then step over the line."

His grandpa tried it, and it worked!

Noah dashed ahead to claim their spot. When Mom and Grandpa caught up, they spread a blanket on the sand. But Noah didn't want to sit.

"Grandpa, I'll race you to the water!" he called.

"Okay," his grandpa said as he fumbled with the buttons on his shirt. "Let's have your mom get us started right after I take my medication."

Noah's mother smiled and waited until his grandpa was ready. Then she said, "On your mark, get set...Go!"

Noah took off and leaped into the ocean. His grandfather couldn't have kept up with him even if he didn't have Parkinson's. Noah was too excited and too fast!

All day they had a blast. Grandpa taught Noah how to build a castle in the sand, how to fly a kite in the air, and how to balance on a boogie board in the water.

Late in the afternoon, Noah's grandpa said, "Hey, buddy, how about going for a walk with me?"

As they walked, Noah asked, "Can we race again?"

"Not today," his grandfather replied. "I'm starting to feel a little tired."

Noah felt frustrated. Sometimes he wished things were like they used to be.

"Why don't we look for seashells instead?" his grandpa suggested.

"Okay!" agreed Noah, feeling better already.

"Grandpa," Noah said as he picked up a sand dollar, "why did you get Parkinson's?"

"The doctor isn't sure what causes Parkinson's," his grandpa answered. "It just happened."

"But what made it happen?" Noah asked.

"Well, Parkinson's happens in the brain. Certain parts of my brain have stopped making chemicals that control my body. That can cause problems. Things that used to be easy have become harder."

"Like keeping your hand from shaking? And buttoning your shirt?"

"Right. My brain used to be able to tell my body how to move, and my body did it," his grandfather explained. "But now, when my brain tells my body to do something, my body doesn't always listen. Like when we were at the end of the boardwalk. My brain was telling my feet to move, but my feet weren't listening."

"But I helped you," Noah said happily.

"You sure did, buddy." His grandfather smiled.

"Does Parkinson's make you have trouble sleeping too?"

"Yes," his grandfather answered. "It's also why I sometimes forget things, don't have a good sense of smell anymore, and sometimes feel too hot or too cold."

"But your medicine helps," Noah said, picking up another shell.

"My medicine helps a lot for some things," his grandfather replied. "And my exercises help for other things. I need both every day."

After a few minutes, Noah asked, "Grandpa, will you get better?"

"Well," his grandfather said, "lots of doctors are trying to find a cure. But everybody with Parkinson's is different. So for now I'll keep trying to do the things that work for me."

"Will Mom or I get Parkinson's?" Noah asked, looking a little worried.

"Probably not. Most people don't. You can't catch it from me like you caught that cold last winter."

Noah and his grandpa stopped to examine a starfish in a small tidal pool. As he was looking at the starfish, Noah asked quietly, "Is it my fault you have Parkinson's? You said it's in your brain, and you hurt your head when you tripped over my toys and fell."

"Oh, buddy!" his grandpa said, giving Noah a big hug. "No, it's not your fault! You didn't make me get Parkinson's. No one did. It's just one of those things that happens."

"Okay, Grandpa." Noah smiled.

Just then, his grandpa's watch beeped. "Time for my medication again," he said.

Grandpa took his medicine and he and Noah walked back to their spot on the beach to decorate their sand castle with the seashells they had found.

At the end of the day, Noah helped his mom and grandpa pack up.

"This was the best beach day!" he said. "Can we do it again tomorrow?"

Mom and Grandpa laughed.

"Maybe not tomorrow, buddy," said his grandpa. "But we'll come back soon."

"Hooray!" shouted Noah.

They all laughed and headed back, with Noah leading the way.

A Note about Parkinson's

Imagine when Noah's grandfather was a little boy and someone wanted to get more information about Parkinson's. After the doctor explained everything, folks went home and tried to make sense of what they had just heard. There was no Internet, few advocacy groups, and no medical websites to read to better understand the symptoms and the doctor's unwieldy terminology.

Bradykinesia, a symptom associated with Parkinson's, wasn't in the family encyclopedia. There was no National Parkinson Foundation website to remind us that bradykinesia refers to the slowed and stiff movement often seen with Parkinson's. It wasn't easy to find reliable explanations about other common symptoms like rhythmic tremors at rest, posture and balance problems, shaky and small handwriting, softer voice, diminished facial expressions, or the sudden inability to start or continue walking (known as freezing).

Many people in Noah's grandfather's generation also had limited information about the underlying brain dysfunction that caused their symptoms. Not knowing why the body is exhibiting these changes can make living with Parkinson's needlessly more difficult. However, today we have access to resources that distill decades of research explaining the causes of Parkinson's symptoms. Not only can we read about how genetics can play a role in the development of the disorder, but we can also access videos illustrating how the loss of neurons in specific regions of the brain causes particular symptoms.

Today, we can easily educate ourselves about medication options for treatment, learn about the importance of rest and exercise, or explore possible surgical treatments. Through advocacy groups, such as the Michael J. Fox Foundation for Parkinson's Research, we can find numerous ways to connect with other families who are coping with Parkinson's. The shared under-standing and sense of community provided by these modern resources can be a great comfort.

The following websites are excellent resources to get information and support for Parkinson's:

- The Michael J. Fox Foundation for Parkinson's Research is one of the largest advocacy, informational, and fund-raising organizations for those dealing with Parkinson's. www.michaeljfox.org
- The National Parkinson Foundation also provides education, support, and fund-raising. www.parkinson.org

Nicholas Jasinski, PsyD
Clinical Neuropsychologist

How to Talk to Children about Parkinson's

- Engage in an open, honest conversation and encourage questions from children. Know that a child's questions and concerns can change as she gets older and as a loved one's Parkinson's progresses. It's important to keep the conversation going throughout the years.

- Explain Parkinson's and its symptoms in simple terms so children can easily absorb the information.

- Because children tend to take many cues from those around them, remember to model positive thinking by engaging in positive behavior and actions when discussing Parkinson's.

- Find a way to look at the lighter side of Parkinson's. Laughing about some symptoms and little problems that may come up is okay. Doing so will help make Parkinson's seem less scary for children.

- Let children know that they are part of the Parkinson's team and that the whole family will be working together to help one another. Talk with children about how they can help a loved one with Parkinson's. If the person is okay with accepting help, a child can assist with daily tasks that have become difficult for the person to accomplish on his own.

- Make sure children know Parkinson's is not their fault. Children sometimes think they cause bad things to happen because of something they said, did, or even thought. A child might think Parkinson's is her fault because she was mad or behaved badly. Let her know this is not the case.

- Remind children that even though a person with Parkinson's may not be able to do everything he once could, children are still loved exactly the same.

For additional resources, please visit www.albertwhitman.com.